A Safe Place in the Country

Story by Pamela Rushby
Illustrations by Chiara Fedele

Contents

Author's Note

In 1939, at the beginning of World War II,
the British government made a plan to move children far away from British cities that were in danger of being bombed.

Over three days, thousands of schoolchildren and their teachers travelled by trains, buses and boats to safe places out in the country.
They were placed in private homes.

The children often didn't know where they were going, who they would stay with or when they would go home again.

These were some of the British children who were moved to the country in September 1939, before World War II began.

Chapter 1

A Plan to Leave London

Late one evening, Kenny came downstairs for a drink of water. He stopped on the stairs. His mum and dad were talking. Kenny listened.

"It's called 'Operation Pied Piper'," his dad said to his mum. "The government wants to move schoolchildren and their teachers out of London. They want to send them to safe places in the country before the war starts."

"How soon do they want to do this?" asked Kenny's mum, her voice shaking.

"Very soon," said his dad. "The question is, should we send Kenny and Brenda away?"

"They're only nine and five," said Kenny's mum. "I don't like to send them away without us. But maybe we should, if they'll be safer in the country."

Kenny froze. The country? By themselves? He'd never been to the country before. All he knew was that there were trees and animals and small villages.

He didn't want to go and leave his mum and dad. He especially didn't want to go with his little sister, Brenda. She could be a pest, sometimes.

"They should go. Then we'll know they are safe," said Kenny's dad.

Kenny gulped. He backed quietly up the stairs. Like it or not, it seemed as though Kenny and Brenda were going to the country.

Chapter 2

Marching to the Station

Things moved quickly. Just a few days later, Kenny, Brenda and their mum walked to the school gate. There, they met a group of other students and their parents. The teachers were there, too.

Each child carried a bag with a change of clothes, a toothbrush, a comb and a facecloth. Labels with their name, address and school were pinned to their coats. They had been told to bring enough sandwiches to last all day.

The teachers formed the children into a line. Mr Waverley, the head teacher, stepped to the front. He carried a sign with the words "Lambeth Primary School" on it.

LAMBETH
PRIMARY SCHOOL

"Let's go to the station!" Mr Waverley shouted.

Brenda clutched at Kenny's coat. Kenny tried to shake her off, but she wouldn't let go.

Some of the children started to cry.

"Now, now," said Mr Waverley. "No tears. Let's sing a song instead!"

"What will we sing?" a girl asked.

"'The Lambeth Walk', sir?" suggested Kenny. It was his favourite song because Lambeth was the part of London where they lived. He also liked it because he got to shout "Oi!" loudly at the end.

"Why not?" said Mr Waverley.

They marched off towards the train station.
Their parents followed, to wave goodbye.

The children stopped crying, and laughed, as Mr Waverley sang, "*You'll find yourself, doing the Lambeth Walk – oi!*"

At the station, some volunteers who were helping with Operation Pied Piper hurried the children and their teachers towards a waiting train.

Kenny's mum put Brenda's hand in his.
"Be good," she told them. "Don't complain if things aren't quite what you're used to. Most importantly – don't get separated. I'm depending on you, Kenny, to stay with your sister."

"All right," Kenny said.

Kenny and Brenda followed the other children and their teachers onto the train.

The teachers started to sing another song as the train pulled out of the station. The song was called "Keep the Home Fires Burning". Now, it was the parents left standing on the station platform who cried.

Chapter 3

Staying Together

Kenny stared out the window of the train. Soon, instead of houses, shops and factories, he was looking at green fields, sheep and cows. There were very few houses and very few people.

"Is this the country?" Brenda asked.

"It must be," Kenny answered.

In the late afternoon, the train stopped at a small station.

"We get off here," Mr Waverley called. "We have to go to the village hall."

"Are we staying here, miss?" Kenny asked his teacher, Miss Green.

"Yes, Kenny, we'll stay with families here in Brockden," Miss Green answered.

Brockden
Station

At the village hall, no one seemed to know which child was to stay with which family. A lady with a clipboard tried to sort everyone out. The children stood in a line as people from Brockden came in and looked at them.

A woman smiled at Brenda. “Isn’t she sweet?” she said to the lady with the clipboard. “I can take her.”

Kenny gulped. “You’ll need to take me too, then,” he said. “She’s my sister.”

“I’m sorry,” the woman said. “I haven’t room for two children.”

A few minutes later, a farmer came in.

"I'll take that lad," he said, pointing at Kenny. "He can help with the cows."

Cows! Kenny wasn't happy. "Would you take my sister too?" he asked.

"No," said the farmer. "I couldn't look after a little girl."

"I'm sorry," said the lady with the clipboard to Kenny and Brenda. "But it looks like you'll just have to be separated."

Kenny didn't know what to do. He had promised his mum that they would stay together.

Just then, another lady hurried into the hall. "I'm sorry," she called. "I was held up sorting mail at the post office!"

"Miss Bertram, I'm so glad to see you," said the lady with the clipboard. "Kenny and Brenda want to stay together. Can you take two children?"

"Well, I was only meant to have one, but I suppose I could have two," said Miss Bertram.

"Kenny, Brenda," called the lady with the clipboard. "This is Miss Bertram, our postmistress. You'll be staying with her."

"Both of us?" Kenny asked. He wanted to be sure.

"Yes, I'm taking both of you," said Miss Bertram, smiling at them. "Let's go home!"

Chapter 4

A New Home in the Country

Miss Bertram lived in a cottage just outside the village.

"You've got grass for a roof!" said Brenda.

Miss Bertram laughed. "The grass is called thatch," she said.

In the backyard, Miss Bertram had chickens, a pig in a sty and two goats.

"Maybe you can learn to milk the goats," Miss Bertram said to Kenny.

At least they're not as big as cows! thought Kenny.

"And perhaps Brenda could collect the chickens' eggs for me," said Miss Bertram.

"Ooh, yes!" Brenda said.

Kenny and Brenda shared a room, tucked up under the thatched roof. They climbed stairs, steep as a ladder, to get there.

The next day, Kenny and Brenda went to their new school. There wasn't enough room in the Brockden school for all the children from London as well as the village children. So, the village children went in the morning and the city children went in the afternoon.

Kenny was pleased to see his London classmates. They told each other where they were living. Tommy was staying with a family who owned the butcher shop. Jimmy was on a farm. He'd had to help with the cows that morning, but he said it was all right. Lily was staying with the village teacher.

"She said she'll teach me how to play the piano!" Lily said.

For their writing lesson, Miss Green gave each child a postcard.

"In your very best writing," she said, "write to your parents and tell them your new address. Then we'll go to the post office and post them."

Kenny felt worried as he posted his card at Miss Bertram's post office. The war hadn't even begun yet. How long would he and Brenda be away? Would they ever go home again? And would his parents even get the postcard?

Miss Bertram saw his face. "Don't worry, Kenny," she said. "The Royal Mail will always be delivered!"

Chapter 5

A Letter from London

A few weeks went by. The war had begun. There was fighting and bombing in Europe, but not in England. Not yet.

In Brockden, Brenda loved collecting the chickens' eggs. Kenny learned to milk a goat. They paddled in streams, played in green fields and explored the woods around the cottage together. Brenda still followed Kenny everywhere, but she didn't seem to be such a pest any more.

Kenny thought the country was all right, but he missed his London home. Sometimes, after they had gone to bed, Brenda missed her mum, and Kenny had to tell her it was all right and that they would go home – some day.

Miss Bertram must have understood how they were feeling. One night, after Kenny and Brenda had gone to bed, she wrote a letter to their parents.

Soon, a letter arrived from London. It was from Kenny and Brenda's parents.

They wrote that they missed the children, but they were happy Kenny and Brenda were safe in the country. And – guess what? Miss Bertram had invited them to come and visit Brockden. They would be coming the next weekend. They wrote that they couldn't wait to meet Miss Bertram, and see Brenda collecting eggs and Kenny milking a goat.

We heard you made sure Brenda stayed with you, Kenny, they wrote. *We are so proud of you.*

Kenny and Brenda grinned at each other. They quite liked being together now. And they felt safe with Miss Bertram. They couldn't wait to show the country to their parents.